E
YOL

Yolen, Jane.

Meet the monsters.

$16.85

000029236
12/04/1997

DATE			
	WITHDRAWN		

BAKER & TAYLOR

Meet the Monsters

JANE YOLEN AND
HEIDI E. Y. STEMPLE

ILLUSTRATIONS BY
PATRICIA LUDLOW

Walker and Company ✺ **New York**

HAVE YOU EVER MET A MONSTER?

Have you ever met a monster?
No—of course you haven't.
There are no such things as monsters
Except in our imaginations.

But sometimes it is fun
to be just a LITTLE scared.

And sometimes it is fun
to know a bit about all the monsters
who have lived in other people's nightmares.
Because sometimes those nightmares
are our very own.

It is also important to know
how to get rid of the monsters
that live in our nightmares
and in our imaginations
and under our beds
and behind the closet door.
Just in case.
Just in case.
Just in case . . .

                    they are real.

VAMPIRE

So you have just met a vampire
and you think he is dead.
Dead but not dead. Undead.
That's a vampire all right.

He drinks blood.
Your blood—if you are not careful.
From your neck where the big vein beats
under your chin.
The jugular.
And then you will become a vampire, too.
Dead but not dead. Undead.
And stuck at whatever age you are:
seven or seventy-seven or a hundred and seven.
Forever.

Well, maybe not forever.
Vampires CAN be killed.
Daylight makes them turn to dust.
They can be burned up.
A wooden stake through the heart
of a sleeping vampire
kills him dead.
Completely.

And you can always scare a vampire off
by holding up a cross.
Or by wearing a necklace of garlic.
Or by eating garlic.
Or by hanging garlic all around your room.

Of course garlic will scare away your friends, too.
Which is fine—if one of them happens to be a vampire.

WEREWOLF

What's big and hairy, has large teeth,
and changes shape at the full moon?
Give up?
A werewolf.
Or, if you live in Russia, a werebear.
Or, in Africa, a wereleopard.
Or, in India, a weretiger.
Weretigers and leopards
and bears, oh my!

Some people become werewolves by putting on a wolfskin belt.
Some by being under a witch's spell.
And some by being bitten by a werewolf.
Then the full moon comes out and they get all hairy.
Their eyebrows grow together. And they howl at the moon.

To tell if you might be a werewolf,
check your hands.
If your third finger is lots and lots longer
than all your other fingers,
if your eyebrows meet over your nose—
watch out!

There are ways to escape a werewolf.
You can cross a running stream of water
because a werewolf cannot follow you there.
You can hang mistletoe over your door.
But to kill a werewolf takes a silver bullet through the heart,
which means you need a good aim.
A very good aim.

MEDUSA

Medusa is so ugly.
How ugly?
Well, for one thing, she has snakes for hair.
And two boar tusks.
She is so ugly, one look at her
and you will turn to stone.

Are you curious?
Are you starting to turn and . . .
No! Stop! Don't look!
Unless you have a great urge
to be a statue.

In order to kill Medusa,
you must cut off her head.
This is not easy
if you can't look at her.

But, if you use a mirror to see where she is,
you can find her all right.
Be sure to bring a sack along
so you can stick her head in without peeking at it.
Because even dead, she is still ugly.
And even dead, she can still turn you to stone!

If you would rather not see her at all, carry a weasel or a rooster
when you travel in the Libyan desert.
Weasels aren't afraid of her. They will attack her.
And she hides when she hears a rooster crowing.
Even ugly Medusa is afraid of something.

MUMMY

A real mummy is a dead body
that has not decayed.
Yechhhhh.
Some mummies were made
by wrapping dead people in bandages
made of cotton or linen
and filling the people with chemicals.
We call this "embalming."
Lots of people all over the world
made mummies of their dead relatives
or their dead heroes
or their dead kings.
Yechhhhh.

But monster mummies don't stay dead.
They walk about trailing their bandages
in the dirt and in the mud,
looking for the robbers
who broke into their tombs
and stole away the treasures
buried with them.
Yechhhhhhhh.

So if you meet a mummy
and you haven't any treasure—don't worry.
Or else give it right back.
I would.

ABOMINABLE SNOWMAN

On the tallest mountain in the world
lives the Yeti.
He is a snowman.
But he is not made of snow.
He is made of bones and skin and hair.
Lots of hair!

He is eight feet tall
with great big feet
and looks like a human, only hairier.
He likes the cold.
He likes the snow.
But one thing he doesn't like—people.
Some say he is shy.
Some say he is mean.
Some say he is abominable.
Everyone says he is scary!

He has cousins all over the world
with names like Bigfoot and Sasquatch.

But should you come upon a Yeti,
don't be scared.
He may be big
and hairy and ugly,
but he is not very smart.
Just pick up
    a bunch of sticks and stones
    and throw them
    at the Yeti
one at a time.
He loves to catch things
but doesn't like to drop them.
When his arms are full,
    you must run away.
        Run far far away.

SPHINX

If you want to go to Thebes, you will have to pass the Sphinx.
The Sphinx has the head of a woman,
the body of a lion,
and the wings of a bird.
She's a regular carnivore, too.
That means she eats flesh.
Human flesh.
And she doesn't care how old the human is.

There is only one way to get by the Sphinx.
You must answer her riddle.
But, be careful.
You are not going to get a second chance.

Here's her riddle. Are you ready to try?
"What walks first with four feet,
then two feet,
and finally with three feet?"

Do you know the answer?
Don't take too long.
Quick! Here's a hint!
The answer is: a human.
A baby crawls
on two hands and two knees.
In Sphinx riddle talk
that means four legs.
Then a grown-up walks on two legs.
Finally an old person may use a cane.
Three legs.
Whew. You answered just in time.
The Sphinx will not eat you.
Instead, she will fling herself
off the cliff and die.

GOLEM

Too many chores to do?
Why not make a Golem.
You will need a lot of clay—special clay—
clay untouched by human hands.
And you must write God's holy name
on a piece of paper
and put it under the Golem's tongue.

Then Golem can help you
with all of your chores.
He can wash the dishes on Sunday.
He can take out the garbage on Monday.
He can clean your room on Tuesday
and do the laundry on Wednesday.
He can work every day except Saturday.
Golem is a Jewish monster.
He cannot work on the Sabbath.

If you forget and make him work Saturday,
he will break down walls,
he will tear down cities,
he will make an awful mess.
Boy—will you be in trouble!

There are only two ways to stop Golem.
You can reach under his tongue
and take out the paper.
If you are not quite that brave,
you can corner Golem
at the top of a tall building or a high cliff
and push him off.
He will break into a million pieces.
After all, he is just made of clay.

FRANKENSTEIN'S MONSTER

Have you ever felt lonely?
Have you ever thought people were staring at you?
Have you ever had a bad hair day?
It makes you feel mean. And angry.
Ready to throw things around.

Victor Frankenstein made a monster
that felt that way.
Nobody liked him.
Everybody stared at him.
Every day for him
was a bad hair day.
He felt ugly.
You'd feel ugly too,
if you had been made like a patchwork quilt,
with bits and pieces of dead people
all sewn together;
if you had yellow-green skin
and wore a size 21 shoe.

So if you see Frankenstein's monster
coming after you,
mean and angry and lonely,
get out the torches.
He hates torches.
Or—if you are feeling really brave—
be his friend and invite him home for dinner.
He's never been to anyone's home.
At least not for dinner.

LOCH NESS MONSTER

Splish.
Did you hear something?
Splash.
Something behind you?
Something twenty feet big
with a ladder-long neck?
Something with humps and bumps?
Something with a five-foot, lanky, snakey tail?

I bet that something is
the Loch Ness Monster,
who lives in this
Scottish lake:
in the peat dark,
deep dark,
steep dark waters of Ness.
Splish. Don't be afraid.
Splash. Just turn slo-o-o-o-ow-ly.
Focus and . . . she'll disappear.
Nessie is afraid of only one thing . . .
a camera!
Just point it at her and click!
Splash!

ZOMBIE

A zombie is a dead body
that has no soul
and has forgotten he is dead.
What a thing to forget!
He walks around slowly,
staring straight ahead,
and works for his master
in the fields.

The voodoo sorcerer
who stole the zombie from his grave
can make the zombie do wicked things.
Or he can make the zombie
work day and night in the fields.
No wonder the zombie
would rather be dead!
So if you want to give the zombie
back his death,
do this:
Strangle him.
Poison him.
Oh—you don't want to get that close?
Good choice.

There is a better way.
Make the zombie eat salt.
Offer him pretzels.
Give him potato chips.
Feed him French fries.
Then he will remember he is dead.
And die.

GARGOYLE

If you walk along a city street
and something wet hits you,
look up.
If there is no rain falling,
if there are no birds flying,
you have been hit
by gargoyle spit.
Look down.
Gargoyles squat
on the ledges
and the edges
of big city buildings,
especially cathedrals.
And if you have never seen ugly,
look up.
If a gargoyle sees you looking,
it will pretend it is stone.
It will sit still as concrete.
Look down.
You may see the shadow of a gargoyle
thumbing its nose or sticking out its tongue
or scratching itself in nasty places.
Look out!

OGRE AND OGRESS

Ogres are big.
Ogresses, too.
Big as oxcarts when they are young.
Big as houses when they are old.
Big.
And ugly.
With ugly personalities, too.
They live in hovels.
They sleep on dirt.
Boy—do they need baths.
Worst of all,
they like to eat people.
They like people burgers,
and people meatloaf,
and especially people pizza.
But ogres are dumb.
Ogresses, too.
So if YOU can count up to five,
you are already smart enough
to escape from an ogre.
Or an ogress.
Whichever.

WINDIGO

So here we are in the north woods.
The birds are singing.
Little squirrels and rabbits
run across the paths
under the fir trees.
What a pretty place.
What a lovely spot.

NOT.

Something is behind us.
Crick-crack.
The branches snap.
Crash-crush.
Trees are thrown down.
The horrible windigo is coming.
The windigo with his heart of ice.
He loves to eat people,
especially people
out in the woods
where the Ojibway hunters roam.

But you must do what the Ojibways do.
Take a candle and melt it down to tallow.
When you see the windigo, say:
"Open wide and I'll jump inside."
Then pour the hot wax down his throat.
It will melt his heart of ice
and he'll be your friend in the woods
forever.

SO YOU'VE MET THE MONSTERS

Next time you are in your bed
and the night light has burned out,
if you hear something move
under the bed,
in the closet,
down the hall—
you KNOW what to do.
You tell yourself this is all for fun.
This is just in your imagination.
Then you get out your garlic,
or the salty chips,
or the mistletoe,
or the weasel . . .
just in case.

To our monster, Maddison Jane —J. Y.
who kicked me while we wrote this book —H. E. Y. S.

To my family, especially James and Lance; to Lupin, who always sits patiently whilst I am working;
and for Khon Khen, who used to do the same —P. L.

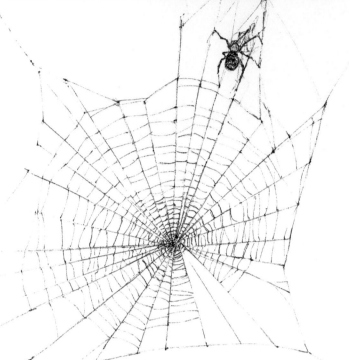

Text copyright © 1996 by Jane Yolen and Heidi E. Y. Stemple
Illustrations copyright © 1996 by Patricia Ludlow

First published in the United States of America in 1996 by Walker Publishing Company, Inc.
Published simultaneously in Canada by Thomas Allen & Son Canada, Limited, Markham, Ontario
Library of Congress Cataloging-in-Publication Data
Yolen, Jane.
Meet the monsters/Jane Yolen and Heidi E. Y. Stemple; illustrations by Patricia Ludlow.
p. cm.
Summary: Children face an assortment of imaginary, literary, and mythical monsters, armed
with information on what they look like and how to get rid of them.
ISBN 0-8027-8441-0 (hardcover). —ISBN 0-8027-8442-9 (reinforced)
[1. Monsters—Fiction.] I. Stemple, Heidi E. Y. II. Ludlow, Patricia, ill. III. Title.
PZ7.Y78Mc 1996
[E]—dc20   96-15126
                                                                              CIP
                                                                              AC
Book design by Eleen Cheung

Printed in Hong Kong

2 4 6 8 10 9 7 5 3 1

BOOKS WE USED FOR RESEARCH

THE BOOK OF BEASTS, by T. H. White. London: Jonathan Cape, 1954.

MYTHOLOGICAL CREATURES, by Paulita Sedgewick. New York: Holt, Rinehart and Winston, 1974.

VAMPIRES, WEREWOLVES AND GHOULS, by Bernhardt J. Hurwood. New York: Ace Books, 1968.

WEREWOLVES AND OTHER MONSTERS, by Thomas G. Aylesworth. Reading, Mass: Addison-Wesley, 1971.

VAMPIRES AND OTHER GHOSTS, by Thomas G. Aylesworth. Reading, Mass: Addison-Wesley, 1972.

MUMMIES, by Georgess McHargue. Philadelphia: J. P. Lippincott Co., 1972.

THE MYSTERY AND LORE OF MONSTERS, by C. J. S. Thompson. New York: Bell Publishing, 1968.

MONSTERS, by Leonard Wolf. San Francisco: Straight Arrow Books, 1974.

THE IMPOSSIBLE PEOPLE, by Georgess McHargue. New York: Holt, Rinehart and Winston, 1972.

MONSTERS, GIANTS, AND LITTLE MEN FROM MARS, by Daniel Cohen. New York: Dell Books, 1975.

WEREWOLVES, by Nancy Garden. Philadelphia: J. P. Lippincott Co., 1973.

FUNK AND WAGNALL STANDARD DICTIONARY OF FOLKLORE, MYTHOLOGY, AND LEGEND, edited by Maria Leach. New York: Funk and Wagnall, 1972.